MEGALODON APOCALYPSE

ERIC S. BROWN

SEVERED PRESS
HOBART TASMANIA

MEGALODON APOCALYPSE

ISBN: 978-1-925342-81-9

MEGALODON APOCALYPSE

2022 had been the year the world had changed. Jack was only fifteen when it all happened. No one really knew what caused the floods. The whackos labeled it an effect of global warming. Others believed we were betrayed by the sun itself—a massive coronal ejection of some kind that reached the Earth and tore through its atmosphere. Still others blamed everything from nuclear war to God. The world had been at war when the floods came, and there had been nuclear strikes. The only explanation which Jack could rule out entirely was God. God had promised never to flood the Earth again. His father had taught him that.

His father had been a good man. He had worked his entire life as a journalist, traveling the globe and providing for his family. Jack remembered the long hours of waiting for his father to come home from work and the closeness that followed when he did. Jack's father always kept in touch even when he was away. The two of them would chat daily via the web. In the end, it was his father who had saved him.

When the rains began, no one imagined that the Earth would be engulfed by them. In fact, most were happy to see them as the area where Jack's family lived, like many others, was in a long drought. Jack and his mother were evacuated from their home after the third straight day of rain. They were soon after evacuated again from the center they had been taken to. It was then that his mother had received a strange call from his dad. His dad had warned that the rains weren't going to be stopping, and he had secured them a spot aboard a ship that was leaving dock from the coast of North Carolina in two days. His mother had moved mountains to get them there in time, and though it cost her life to do so, she got Jack aboard the ship.

Jack had grown onboard the USS Triton, a carrier vessel which had taken on a large number of civilian refugees fleeing the vanishing main lands. He had learned how to fish, the processes for converting salt water to drinking water, and all the basics of survival in the new world that was being born, including how to defend himself. The oceans were full of pirates and raiders. Not even large military vessels proved completely safe from them as time wore on.

He'd been there when Admiral Campbell had gathered *The Fleet,* and the fleet had been his home ever since. Jack was nineteen now and a man. He had worked his way up to command of one of the Fleet's fishing patrols. He was good at his job. The small group of fishing vessels that he led was among the best in the Fleet. They regularly not only met their quotas but surpassed them. The ecological changes the world was continuing to undergo, and the new, desperate need for fish as a source of food had devastated some areas in terms of fishing, but like the Native Americans of the past, the Fleet merely followed its food supply across the waves.

It wasn't just the human race that was adapting to a new nomadic lifestyle; sea life was changing too. Mutations were commonplace. Whole new species of life were born from the planet Earth's climate change. Names like "giant squid" took on a wildly different meaning when compared to the size they had in the world before. There were many of the new lifeforms that actually hunted groups of survivors like the Fleet. The most dangerous of them all were the Megalodons. Life at sea was a tough and demanding one.

If there were any real land masses left, the Fleet hadn't found them in ten years of searching. La Rinconada was one of the last places Jack had heard of officially being absorbed by the rising waters, though for a time it had served as a trading center where various ships and fleets came to trade. The message from it had been several years back, and Admiral Campbell had never taken the Fleet back there again after that message had been received. Soil was one of the most valuable commodities in the world. Farming now was done aboard ships inside specially built holds and on manmade rigs designed especially for the task.

After the rains that flooded and changed the world finally subsided, the weather had become erratic and unpredictable. It had taken time to learn the new ebb and flow of how the world spun. And today Jack saw was going to be a nice day as he stood in the bow of his ship, the Leery, looking out at the blue waters that stretched into the horizon in all directions.

"Gonna be a good one," Hank said, joining Jack where he stood.

Jack laughed. "We could use one. We're behind this week and got some tonnage we need to make up in the cargo hold. I mean, we've got a rep to live up to, you know?"

Hank smiled back at him. "Aye, captain, that we do."

Jack's fishing group consisted of his ship, *The Lost,* and two other vessels, *The Hayden* and *The Shiny Lady.* They were spread out in a wedge formation and awaiting Jack's orders on how to deploy for the day's fishing.

Seaman Gunter came running up to where Jack and Hank stood.

"Captain! We have a surface contact approaching from the north!" Gunter told them.

A pair of binoculars dangled from a cord around Jack's neck. He raised them to his eyes, squinting against the rays of the early morning sun, trying to get a visual on the contact his men on lookout in the ship's tower had reported. At first, he couldn't see anything but what appeared to be open water. Then he saw it and realized it was bobbing up and down in the water and wasn't continuously visible. A giant fin protruding from the ocean's surface and closing fast on his small group of ships. From the size of it, Jack knew they were in trouble.

"Megalodon," he said, voicing the name of the distant creature.

Both Hank and Gunter flinched at the word. Every sailor in the Fleet knew just how dangerous the monsters were. The fishing vessels of the group were armed. No sane captain piloted a ship without some means of defense in this new age of humanity, but they were mainly armed against pirates and raiders. There had been no previous reports of Megalodon activity in the area, or Jack would never have picked this spot for his fishing run. The main fleet was over two days away at maximum speed. Even if they called for help and speed boats were dispatched to come to their aid, it would take them hours to reach their current position.

Jack sprang into action. "Pass word to the other ships. All hands to battle stations! If this thing wants a piece of us, let's at least not make it easy for it."

Running as fast as he could, Jack headed for *The Lost's* bridge. Hank and Gunter followed after him. The bridge was a small one, and so three men crowded in to join Wade, the comm officer/radar tech, and Desju, the navigator, who were already present.

"She's coming in towards *The Shiny Lady,* sir," Wade reported. "At present speed, she'll make contact in just under two minutes. Captain Fal reports her men are prepared and lined up along the ship's portside. She promises she'll, and I quote, "bloody that bastard for us.""

Jack smiled. The Fleet needed more captains like Fal. Why she hadn't been promoted in the Fleet's battle units yet baffled him. The woman had a backbone of steel and the determination to get things done no matter the cost.

"Good," Jack nodded at Wade. "Keep your eyes glued to radar screen, Wade. We can't afford to lose track of the Megalodon if Fal fails to take it out."

Jack knew that even Fal didn't have a snowball's chance in Hell of stopping one of those creatures with the weapons at her disposal, but there was no need point that out to the frightened men around him.

Stepping closer to the bridge's forward window, Jack raised his binoculars again to watch the carnage unfold with his own eyes rather than wait for reports from Wade as they came in.

The early dawn was lit by a barrage of automatic weapons fire as nearly the entire crew of *The Shiny Lady* opened up at the great beast approaching the ship. Clearly, Fal had been holding out on him when it came to her inventory lists, because Jack saw a RPG fly from *The Shiny Lady* towards the Megalodon. The great beast wasn't slowed at all by the fury that met it. The water churned as the RPG struck its surface, but there was no way to tell how badly the RPG had injured the creature, if at all.

The Megalodon slammed into *The Shiny Lady* like an angry fist making contact with plaster. *The Shiny Lady* rocked on the water. Jack could see the distant forms of the men and women of its crew being flung over the deck railing into the waves from the beast's impact. An entire section of *The Shiny Lady's* hull caved inward and Jack imagined the amount of water that must be pouring into her. Unless *The Lost* and *The Hayden* fared better against the monster, Jack knew there was no point in Fal ordering her crew to abandon ship. They would only be stuck in lifeboats to wait for the monster to circle round and have them as an after dinner snack once it was done with the other two ships of the fishing group.

The Hayden had shifted its course and was making a run for it, her engines at full.

"What the . . .?" Jack whirled on Wade, staring at the comm officer. "What is Philip doing? I didn't order him to break formation!"

"I . . . I don't know, sir!" Wade shouted in the enclosed space of *The Lost's* bridge. "He's not responding to my attempts to reach him."

"Coward," Hank spat. "I told you that idiot was never fit for command."

Before Jack could reply, Wade cut in. "The Megalodon has resurfaced from its run on *The Shiny Lady* sir. It appears to be going after *The Hayden!*"

"Bring us about!" Jack ordered. "Full speed."

"We can't overtake that thing," Hank pointed out.

"And we're not trying to," Jack explained. "It's going after *The Hayden* because she looks weak. When it's done and turns around, we'll be there waiting for it."

Jack moved next to Wade at the comm Station, clicked on the ship's intercom, and started barking orders to his crew. "All hands report to the bow. It's our turn to take a shot at that thing!"

"Hank, you have the bridge," Jack said, and started to leave the bridge.

"No freaking way are you going out there to take a shot at that thing without me," Hank protested.

Jack sighed, not having time to argue. "Fine. Gunter, the bridge is yours until we get back. Try not to get my ship sunk."

Jack and Hank made a quick stop at *The Lost's* armory. Jack broke out the ship's sole fifty caliber weapon. "Help me with this thing!" he ordered Hank. The two of them lugged the large gun to the ship's bow where the rest of crew, each armed with everything from shotguns to AK-47s, were already in position.

In the time it took the two men to get the fifty caliber set up and in place, the Megalodon had laid waste to *The Hayden*. The giant shark hadn't rammed *The Hayden* once and left her to sink as it did *The Shiny Lady*. It had hit *The Hayden* over and over until she'd broken apart. Jack cursed himself, feeling responsible though he knew he wasn't. A part of him hoped there was a special place in Hell for cowards like Captain Philip. If *The Hayden* would have only responded to Wade's attempt to reach it, even after Philip had made a run for it, *The Lost* and *The Hayden* both might have had a better chance at surviving the day. They could have caught the giant shark between them and hit it together. Now, *The Lost* would be facing the monster alone, and *The Hayden* was simply gone.

Jack's breath caught in his throat as he saw the Megalodon coming towards *The Lost.* The creature was even more gigantic than its name implied. He had fought sharks like this one before but never one as large as the monster before him now. He could see its shape clearly beneath the waves as it approached. From snout to the end of its rear fin, it was nearly double the length of *The Lost.* Jack could see, too, the monster's bloodied snout that ripped apart the other ships of his group. As powerful and strong as Megalodons were, even with the mutations that gave them a stronger and denser body structure than any shark would have had in the world before the floods, they were still flesh and blood. Destroying the other two ships, and the fire it had taken in the process, had injured the beast. Jack hoped Fal and her crew had bloodied it enough to matter.

Jack took a deep breath and yelled, "Open fire!"

The fifty caliber weapon jerked and shook in his grasp as it spat a stream of automatic fire into the Megalodon's body. The monster was close enough for Jack to see the bullets making impact and ripping away chunks of the monster's flesh. All around him, his crew fired with courage and desperation, fighting for their lives. The barrage of fire was like a constant pounding of pointblank thunder to his ears. He ignored the pain, though, and kept his aim and rate of fire steady.

As the Megalodon plowed into the bow of *The Lost,* shattering it and raising the entire front of the ship upwards out of the water, Jack was thrown from the deck. He flew through the air to plunge into the water and was sucked down by the giant creature's wake. There was no escape. His tears blended with the salt water around him as it poured into and filled his lungs.

****

Admiral Campbell sat behind the desk in his new office. He was still adjusting to not feeling the waves. Like most of the remaining scattered bits and pieces of the human race, he had spent the last decade on a ship. The stillness of the platform city, known as Dry Dock, creeped him out. The citizens of Dry Dock were long allies of the Fleet. He had visited the city often for trading and political reasons but never had any intention of taking up residence himself until a week ago.

Campbell and the city's leader, Governor Bachman, had been close friends on more than a political level. They shared the vision of reuniting all of humanity and believed that coming together was the only hope of saving the human race from the slow death spiral it seemed locked in.

When Bachman reached out to him, Campbell didn't have a clue that the governor was dying. He had thought it was just another need, born of their alliance, which Bachman wanted to attend to. The pirates in the area around Dry Dock were growing bolder every day. Where their new strength in numbers was coming from neither Campbell nor Bachman had an explanation for. Campbell assumed Bachman wanted the Fleet to engage the pirates and drive them away from this section of the Atlantic.

The Fleet was mobile, surviving on the waves. It was strong, and perhaps the strongest group of its type remaining. The city of Dry Dock was strong as well. Its total population aboard the massive structure numbered in the thousands. The people of Campbell's fleet were warriors and fishermen while Bachman's people were engineers and the closest thing the world had left to real farmers. The alliance between them made perfect sense. Campbell's fleet could bring Dry Dock whatever it needed, and Dry Dock in exchange offered repairs, parts, ammo, and grown fruits and vegetables.

Bachman was eighty-three when he passed with Campbell sitting at his bedside. The man's entire life had been spent using his scientific and engineering skills to help folks adapt to the water planet that the Earth had become. Dry Dock was originally a carrier from the navy of the United States and one of the largest oil rigs ever built. Bachman merged the two into one giant platform city, and he had expanded it even further over the years with materials that Campbell and other sailors delivered to him.

The man's dying request was for Campbell to bring an end to the alliance between the Fleet and Dry Dock by making them one and the same. Bachman prepared those he led for the transition in power before his death, and there was no other moral choice for Campbell to accept Dry Dock into the Fleet as an official part of it. That meant Campbell was forced to give up the waves and take Bachman's place here in the city. It wasn't something Campbell wanted, but he owed Bachman, and the addition of Dry Dock to the Fleet's pool of resources was far too great to pass up. Campbell was sure that Bachman was laughing somewhere up in Heaven as he looked down on his old sailor friend, grounded at last.

Campbell shook his head trying to get himself together and ignore the strange feeling of solidness underneath. He turned his attention back to the report he had been reading on the screen in front of him.

The Fleet's primary fishing flotilla under the command of Captain Jack Henshaw was two days overdue. Campbell knew all of his captains personally. No one in the fleet got promoted without his approval. He liked to think he had made the right decisions when it came to picking people he could trust to do their jobs and ensure the safety of their crews, but he also knew he was human and far from perfect. With Jack, though, that promotion was one of the best choices he made in his career since the world fell apart. Jack was levelheaded, confident, and full of passion. He had grown up on Campbell's own vessel and was a part of his personal crew until he'd given Jack *The Lost*. There was no doubt in Campbell's mind that if Jack was overdue and not reporting in that something bad had befallen the fishing flotilla. He hoped Jack was okay, but as the Fleet's admiral he needed to assume the worst regardless of his faith in Jack's skills as a captain and experienced sailor. The question was what should he do now? The Fleet needed the fish that he entrusted Jack to return with, and there were the lives of the three crews of those fishing vessels to consider as well. Before the mess of taking over Dry Dock that Bachman had left him with, he would have simply taken the entire fleet and headed in the direction of the flotilla's last known coordinates. Being the leader of a fleet instead of a stable city had its advantages. Now, he was forced to consider Dry Dock too. The pirates, while no match head on with the Fleet in terms of numbers and firepower in his opinion, were too dangerous to Dry Dock to be ignored. He couldn't order the Fleet to Jack's last known position. Doing so would leave Dry Dock vulnerable. Dispatching a small task force, though, might be possible but was a risk as well. If they, too, failed to return, it would be more ships and people lost for nothing.

Campbell sighed and rocked back in his chair. There seemed to be no good choice given the new circumstances of his command. He picked up the glass of water on his desk and chugged half of it in a single continuous gulp. Campbell quit smoking years ago, not exactly by choice, but right now his body fell into the old habit of demanding a smoke when he was stressed out. There were cigarettes on Dry Dock, but the cost was high even to someone as powerful as he was. Campbell finished his water hoping it would help curb the craving he felt.

A knock sounded on the door to his office.

"Come," Campbell ordered whoever was outside.

The door opened inward as Captain Martin entered. Her short cropped black hair sharpened the angles of her bird like face. Her uniform was clean and perfectly in order, a rarity among the officers under his command. Usually if an officer was as clean and well dressed as Martin, Campbell would demand to know why they hadn't been working alongside their crew. In Martin's case, though, upon taking command of Dry Dock from Bachman, he appointed her his liaison to the lead engineers, doctors, and scientists aboard the platform, so her appearance fit the work she was assigned to.

"I hope I am not disturbing you, sir," Martin said.

Campbell noticed the stack of folders she carried under her right arm and asked, "More things for me to sign I take it?"

Martin glanced down at the folders she carried and then looked back at him. "Yes, sir, I am afraid so. Even after a week's worth of effort, the Fleet staff assigned to Dry Dock are still far from completing a proper inventory of everything we've just gained by adding all of this city to our resource pool. Not to mention there's much left to be done in terms of deciding which projects Bachman had underway at the time of his death, which need to be shut down, and which need to be sped up in terms of priority."

"And to think, I used to say that Bachman had it easy here compared to all the crap I had to juggle with the Fleet," Campbell laughed. "Making these kinds of calls as an administrator is in some ways a lot different than being an admiral."

"Bachman's faith in your ability to take over here was clear, sir," Martin said, trying to sound encouraging.

He saw Martin glance at the screen of the powered up laptop on his desk.

"No word from Jack and his fisherman I take it," Martin half asked, half stated as she sat down in the chair across the desk from Campbell.

Campbell shook his head sadly. "None at all. I am thinking of dispatching a task force to check up on them."

"That may be a good idea sir. If they don't return soon, we'll need to tap into Dry Dock's onboard supplies to feed the Fleet. You've only been in power here for a week, so such an act might be looked upon badly by the few elements of the city that resent your new position here."

"I hadn't thought of that," Campbell frowned. "But you're right."

"So far we've been lucky in that Bachman did all he could to prepare the people of Dry Dock for the transition in power. Most folks in the city know how close you and Bachman were, and well, to tell the truth, they are sort of relieved you are here. They know you've kept the Fleet functioning and alive all these years, so there's no question as to your competence. A handful of the science folks, though, are deeply afraid that you'll take Dry Dock in a much more militant direction, turning their Athens into a Sparta."

"I can understand that concern," Campbell nodded, "But I am in command now, and they need to understand no matter what I decide."

"I don't think it will come to armed resistance, sir. They're scholars, and we are warriors. They're too smart not to realize that too."

"I hope you're right. Bachman told me about some of the more military stuff his people have on the back burner. If one of those eggheads goes psycho over this. . ."

"I delegated dealing with *those* projects to Captain Rikel," Martin grinned.

"God in heaven help those poor nerds." Campbell smiled at Martin. Rikel was the most vicious and hardnosed commander the Fleet had. Martin assigning him to the task of overlooking and/or shutting down the few weapons projects onboard the platform was the perfect choice. Everyone in the Fleet feared Rikel. The guy was like some kind of Nazi stormtrooper when it came to enforcing Campbell's will. Campbell didn't often call on Rikel to handle issues in the Fleet despite the man's job of being its head of security, but when he did, he knew whatever it was would be dealt with even if it meant folks missing or in an infirmary that next day.

"Back to the issue you were dealing with though, sir," Martin redirected their conversation. "I suggest giving Captain Stone command of *The Deathdealer, The Hydra, The Striker,* and *The Viper*. Let him take them to check on Jack. That should be more than enough firepower to deal with anything they're likely to run into out there in the direction that Jack's flotilla was at last report. Stone isn't the sort of captain who will balk at retreating if he has to, and *The Viper* is the fastest ship the

Fleet has at its disposal. That will stack the odds in their favor of getting word back to us even if they do run into trouble they can't handle."

"Agreed. Make it so," Campbell waved at hand dismissively at Martin.

"Yes, sir," Martin answered. "Would you like me to just leave these reports and such here for you to look over or stay and brief you on them first?"

Campbell grimaced as he eyed the mass of folders Martin plopped onto the top of his desk then reluctantly growled, "Go on. Jack and his people may already be out of time. I'll manage these myself I guess."

Martin saluted him before she left his office. Campbell watched her go before he shut his laptop and reached for the stack of folders.

****

"You've got be kidding me." Stone glared at Martin. "We just got here a week ago. Some of the ships you just named are undergoing refits while they're in dock. You know that, right?"

Martin shrugged. "Actually, I didn't, and I didn't come here to listen to your problems, captain. You are to have the list of ships I gave you prepared to be out on the waves before nightfall. Those orders come from Admiral Campbell himself."

"Yes, ma'am," Stone shot her a fierce salute.

"Good," Martin said. "I'll leave you to it then."

Stone resisted the urge of flipping her off behind her back as she walked away. The job she just dropped him was nigh impossible given the state of the ship's Campbell had asked for. Such an order made Stone wonder if Campbell's new position was already making him lose touch with the status of the Fleet itself. There was nothing a mere captain like himself could do about it, though, other than follow the orders that were handed to him.

Turning to his men, Stone started barking orders at the top of his lungs. He didn't have a lot of time, and the amount of work ahead of him was staggering.

Three hours later, Stone sat in the command chair aboard *The Viper*. *The Viper* wasn't his ship, but Stone deemed that he needed to be on it in case the task force ran into more trouble than it could handle. He didn't trust anyone but himself in getting word back to Dry Dock and Campbell about whatever might be out there if the task force were compelled into retreat.

The task force was underway with *The Viper* leading it. *The Deathdealer* brought up the task force's rear. It was the heaviest ship of the task force, and while slower than a lot of ships in the Fleet, possessed enough firepower to make its presence worth allowing it to slow them down. *The Deathdealer* was an "old world" battleship crammed from bow to stern with missile launchers and other serious firepower. It even had an intact and functional CIWS. By itself, it could tear the other three ships of the task force to shreds in a matter of minutes. The armor of its hull was covered with the scars of previous battles and looked like a floating junk pile. Such an appearance only added to the ship's lethalness, however. Anyone outside of the Fleet might look at it and mistake it for a barely operational derelict instead of the full out engine of war that it was.

Stone checked and rechecked his data. By his best estimation, Task Force Alpha, as he had named the group of ships under his command, was half a day away from *The Lost's* last known location. They should reach it shortly after daybreak if he kept the task force running at its maximum speed.

Tired and strung out from all the hurried preparations of leaving the city of Dry Dock on such short notice, Stone left the running of the task force to his EXO and closed his eyes where he sat. It wasn't the first time he had slept on the bridge of a ship he commanded, and if he lived through this op, Stone figured it wouldn't be his last either.

****

Lord Dagon arose from the giant bed that took up most of the spacious cabin leaving the four naked women that had surrounded him slumbering. One was thin with jet black hair. One was an equally thin and girlish looking blonde. Another's head was topped with flaming red hair above her well-toned and warrior-like body. The last was a second blonde with large breasts and ample buttocks. The skin of the four women wore a glistening sheen of sweat upon their skin, not all of it from the high humidity of the cabin. Dagan glanced over his shoulder at the women, a smug smile on his face as he moved to where his battle armor rested upon on the room's sole table. The women were his, as were all the women among his followers. Freedom was a detestable and wicked concept, and Lord Dagon played a part in its destruction before the flood. People were sheep and they needed a wolf to lead them if they were to have any hope of survival . . . and he was that wolf.

Piece by piece, he fastened the hardened titanium alloy armor into place and relished the coolness of its touch against his skin. Lord Dagon put on the twisted helmet of the armor last. It covered his face entirely, hiding the scars beneath it from view. The helmet was a grotesque mask that was so well carved it almost looked alive. Its eye slits were filled with red glass that allowed Lord Dagon to see the world as if it were drenched in blood and they caught the light in such a manner that someone looking at him might believe that they glowed. Around the eye slits, the rest of the helmet was a mass of tentacles that were cast to make them appear to be writhing atop his shoulders.

His armor donned, Lord Dagon walked across the cabin to the eighteen-foot by eighteen-foot window that served as its far wall. Through it, he looked down upon his fleet. The ships below him numbered in the dozens, each and every one rigged for war. There was no room for weakness in Lord Dagon's worldview. His own ship, upon which the metal of his metal of his boots clanged as he had walked to the window, was called *The Entropy.* It was the largest vessel under his command. Once it had been a battleship, but Lord Dagon had refitted it over the years to be much faster and leaner than a normal ship its size. Firepower was all well and good, but there was something to be said for coming up alongside your enemy's ship and boarding it. *The Entropy's* bow was pointed like the head of a spear and reinforced to withstand impacts that would tear another ship to shreds. An enemy vessel pierced by its point had never been able to escape Lord Dagon's fury.

Lord Dagon clenched one of his armored hands into a fist as he thought of his enemies. The city of Dry Dock was a continual thorn in his side. The tactics he and his followers used simply did not fare well against such a large and well-populated target. Taking Dry Dock would cost him greatly in terms of ammo and men if he went after it. Worse, there were now rumors among the latest batch of prisoners added to his army in training that the Fleet had joined fully with it and was no longer at prowl on the waves but had made the city their home. The only good part of those rumors was that they also told of Stephen Bachman's passing. That wretched scholar deserved to freeze in the iciness of the deep and feel its cold tendrils about him.

If the stories and rumors were true, Lord Dagon knew that Admiral Campbell of the Fleet would be in power over the city as well. He and Campbell had clashed numerous times, each blooding the other in turn without ever a clear victory in their private war. Aside from Campbell's fleet, there was no other mobile power on the oceans that could challenge Lord Dagon's horde. And that fleet was now combined with the strength of Dry Dock. Still, Lord Dagon knew the city of Dry Dock must be the next target for his horde. They needed the supplies the vast city held. No other target could offer them not only survival, but a city for him to rule as he saw fit.

Lord Dagon tapped the comlink on the side of his helmet, activating it.

"Gather the captains of my fleet," his deep voice rumbled over the comm. "We must lay plans for the taking of Dry Dock at once."

****

Very few in the Fleet knew that many of its ships still possessed homing beacons left over tech from the world before the flood, which enabled a user versed in their operation to use the signal the beacons sent out to hone in on and find any ships that went missing. Only Admiral Campbell and a select group of captains—those who commanded more than one ship—had access to the knowledge that the devices existed and the means to use them. Stone was one of those select few.

"Anything yet?" he asked his EXO, Stanberry.

"We're picking up the signal you told us about just fine, sir, and closing on it fast," Stanberry answered. "ETA in less than an hour."

"Good." Stone nodded and rubbed at his eyes. The sleep he made a point to catch up on during transit had served its purpose. He was rested and his mind clear.

"Keith, any indication of what will be waiting on us when we arrive?" Stone asked his radar tech.

Keith shrugged where he sat at the radar station. "I'm not picking up any vessels in the area if that's what you're asking, sir."

Stone frowned. He had used the homing beacon tech in the past to locate ships that had gone astray before, and it had never failed him. "You're sure about that?"

"Yes, sir," Keith said. "Positive."

"Condition Yellow, all ships," Stone ordered.

"Sir, are we expecting trouble?" Stanberry asked. "Or are you just being cautious?"

"I have always found it better to be prepared than sorry later." Stone turned to glance at where Stanberry stood behind his command chair. "We have no idea what happened to Captain Jack's fishing flotilla. At this point, though, I think it's safe to say whatever happened is more than just some sort of technical trouble they ran into."

"The sheer amount of firepower the admiral loaned out to this task force supports your reasoning, sir," Stanberry agreed. Stanberry was a rail thin man with white, not gray hair. His appearance was odd and sometimes creeped out those new to serving aboard *The Viper*. Stone wasn't among those folks. He had met Albinos before in his life, and Stanberry's appearance didn't faze him at all. What did strike Stone about Stanberry was the man's "by the book" approach to everything. It was ease to see how Stanberry had made it to the rank of captain but had never gone on to the command of more than a single ship. To Stanberry's credit, the man had accepted Stone stepping in and taking over *The Viper* without so much as a veiled offhand remark much less an open complainant. In the hours they had spent together so far, Stone had come to see that Stanberry was about getting the job done and done well no matter the circumstances. He wasn't a glory hound like some of the Fleet's captains could be at times.

"You know this ship better than me, Stanberry," Stone said. "I was thinking of kicking her engine up to full and heading onto *The Lost's* apparent location ahead of the rest of our contingent. Tell me, do you think *The Viper* is up to such a run?"

"Oh, she's ready, sir," Stanberry answered proudly, his love of his ship clear in his voice. "If we run into combat, you have to remember that she was designed for speed, though, sir, not heavy fighting."

"You heard, Keith," Stone reminded his EXO. "Radar isn't showing anything up ahead."

"You are in command of this ship at present, sir, not me. I shall trust your judgement just as Admiral Campbell must."

"Alright then," Stone leaned forward. "Helmsman, kick things up a couple of notches. Keith, let the other ships know what we're up to. I'd hate for them to think they needed to try to keep up," Stone said, and laughed.

Stanberry smirked at Stone's comment.

The Viper's engines roared, and she shot forward, building speed as she went, leaving the rest of the task force behind quickly. It took a mere five minutes for the ship to cover the remaining distance to the area where *The Lost's* beacon was broadcasting from.

Stone ordered the ship to slow as they came in on the area and was glad he did so. The water ahead of the ship was filled with debris according to its lookouts. Standing up from his seat, Stone approached the bridge's window and stared out at the mess that bobbed up and down on the waves.

"By the holy depths," he muttered. Even spread apart by time, the wreckage in the water was easily too much to belong to a single vessel. Stone knew at once that something had engaged the fishing flotilla out here and had torn it to pieces.

"Battle stations, all hands!" Stone shouted. "Keith, full active sweep of this entire area. If there's something out there, I want to know about it."

"Whatever did this is long gone, sir," Keith announced. "My screen is still clear of contacts other than the debris field. I'm only picking it up now due to our proximity."

"Understood." Stone nodded at the radar tech and then turned his attention back to Stanberry. "Thoughts?"

Stanberry appeared as much at a loss as Stone was. "Whoever or whatever hit the flotilla did so hard and fast. At least, that's my guess at any rate. I do not believe it was the pirates that Admiral Campbell is so concerned about though. The pirates would have taken those ships, not destroyed them."

"You're right," Stone said as he thought things over. He snapped his fingers at a nearby yeoman. "Binoculars. Now."

The yeoman ran to fetch a pair that lay on the navigator's console and shoved them into Stone's waiting hands. Stone raised them to his eyes, trying to get a better look at some of the larger pieces of debris that bounced about in the water. There was no sign of charring or fire damage that would have been left from torpedo strikes or the like. For all intents and purposes, the bits of ship out there looked to have been literally shattered as if some overpowering force had rammed into them.

A chill ran down Stone's spine as he put two and two together. "This wasn't the work of pirates. Of that I am sure."

"A Megalodon," Stanberry said before Stone could bring himself to utter the words aloud.

Stone nodded. "Those fishing ships wouldn't have had anything onboard to combat one of those creatures. They would have been armed against boarders. The poor bastards didn't stand a chance."

"The admiral will not be happy," Stanberry sighed. "I am aware that he and Captain Jack were on close terms."

"Not much we can do about that," Stone said sadly. "Bring us to a dead stop. We'll wait on the other ships of the task force here and do a full search for survivors once they arrive."

"There won't be any," Stanberry shook his head.

"We will do a search by quadrants regardless," Stone said more firmly. "If anyone did survive, we're going to give them every chance to stay alive that we can."

"Sir, I have a contact!" Keith shouted. "We've got incoming from the south."

"Pirates?" Stone asked.

"No, sir," Keith said his voice strained with fear. "The contacts are subsurface, sir, and they're massive. Much too large to be approaching at the speed they are to be ships."

"How many?" Stone rasped.

"Their formation is too tight to get a good read on, sir, but I would wager half a dozen at minimum."

"We need to run," Stanberry cut in. "Even if the rest of the task force were with us, engaging that many Megalodons is too great a risk."

Stone wanted to stay and fight. He longed for vengeance on the monsters that had destroyed the ships of the fishing flotilla. He knew, though, that Stanberry was right as he almost always was. If they stayed, they were dead.

"Bring us around, maximum speed. Warn the task force that we're returning, and we have Hell following after us."

****

Lord Dagan sat the head of the long table in *The Entropy's* meeting room. The captains of his ships sat along each side, the lines of their seats stretching down almost all the way to the room's sole entrance. A great, black trident rested against the side of Lord Dagon's chair. It was his preferred weapon and a symbol of dominance over those that followed him. He knew very few of his captains by name and saw no need to develop any relationship with them beyond making sure his will was carried out through their actions. Captains Tyrell and Jaeger were notable exceptions to this. They were his trusted hands. Tyrell sat to his left and Jaeger to his right in the seats next to his own at the head of the table. Tyrell was his enforcer and the muscle that kept the others in line when Lord Dagon himself was not present to do so. Tyrell thrived on pain and torture, so the job was perfect for him. Jaeger, though, was a quiet, smallish man. Thick rimmed glasses covered his eyes below his short cropped hair. If Lord Dagan were ever to name someone in his horde that was above him in intellect, it would be Jaeger. That was one of the reasons he kept Jaeger close. The man's cunning and tactical instincts were uncanny. He was a methodical type and not prone to error. Though Jaeger was capable of making whatever calls a battle called for, his thoughts were always several steps ahead of his enemy, and he didn't care to take to the long road if it meant victory in the end. Tyrell and Jaeger were the only captains who had the freedom to speak without being spoken to in his presence.

"I can only assume that you have called us here to discuss the siege of Dry Dock," Jaeger stated, removing his glasses to clean them with the edge of his uniform's shirt. The fact that Jaeger opted to wear a uniform sat him apart from those around him as well. The cloth of its shirt, pants, and jacket were a dark gray, styled after those of the German SS that were worn in the days of World War II. Lord Dagan knew that Jaeger fancied himself to be such an officer. Lord Dagan's other captains wore everything from the tattered rags of long time seamen to medieval armor like his own.

"Siege?" Tyrell raged. "How dare you suggest that those infidels could hold out against us!"

Lord Dagan raised one of his armored hands, the spikes upon his knuckles catching the light of the candles that lit the meeting room. "Silence," he ordered.

Jaeger shoved his glasses back onto his nose but said nothing more while Tyrell seethed with anger. The two of them never got along. If they did, Lord Dagan knew that it would mean they needed to be disposed of immediately.

"Captain Tyrell, do you have a plan for taking the city of Dry Dock?" Lord Dagan's voice rumbled like thunder inside the meeting room.

"My Lord, I know that the Fleet has joined with Dry Dock but that means nothing. We've bested the ships of the Fleet before and can do again. They may know that we are close by and preparing to strike but know not the hour of our attack or the direction we will come. We must fall upon them with the wind at our backs and wipe them from the face of the waves with a single bold stroke."

Jaeger snorted in the wake of Tyrell's display of bravado. Lord Dagan turned his red eyes upon the smaller man. Jaeger, though, only smiled.

"I take it you disagree, Captain Jaeger?" Lord Dagan challenged him.

"I would disagree with Tyrell's plan if he had one my Lord, but what he is suggesting is not a plan at all. It's merely a wild and suicidal charge at a much larger and better equipped force," Jaeger said calmly.

"Blasphemy!" Tyrell spat. "There is no great power than Lord Dagan's horde upon the waves of this world!"

"Captain Tyrell!" Lord Dagan warned. "Do not make me end the life of one as valuable as yourself."

Tyrell bowed his head, though he still glared at Jaeger as he did so. "Yes, great Lord. Forgive me."

"Tell me your plan, Captain Jaeger," Lord Dagan demanded.

"The merging of Dry Dock and the Fleet is in its birthing stages, my Lord. That can be exploited to our advantage, I think. I suggest slipping some of the men into the city under the guise of merchants or members of the Fleet itself. Have these men plant explosives in some locations I will advise on. The amount of disruption and damage such explosions would do . . . well, they would certainly give us an edge." Jaeger paused to collect his thoughts, and sat up straighter in his chair. "Also, a feint in these circumstances might prove extremely valuable to our cause. If we sent a task force to attack the city in advance, convince the city they are our main force, and have them lure away a great deal of the units of the Fleet now docked at the city, it would lessen their advantages in numbers enough when combined with the explosions to give us an opening to take the city without a siege."

"Do you really believe it would come down to a siege otherwise?" Lord Dagan leaned forward.

Any other man at the table would likely have crapped in his pants at such intense attention from Lord Dagan but not Jaeger.

Jaeger nodded. "I believe so, yes. Their defenses are too many and thickly placed for us to simply plow through. Worse, if it came to a siege, we would lose. We don't have the supplies and resources at our disposal that Dry Dock does. We wouldn't have units who could break away to search for resupply either. They would break us with time. That is a certainty."

Lord Dagan slumped comfortably back into his chair, mulling over what Jaeger suggested. "And this feint? Who would lead it?"

"Why, Captain Tyrell, of course," Jaeger beamed.

"You would have us attack those fools only to run?" Tyrell growled, and then caught himself. He looked up at Lord Dagan and shut his mouth.

"Only Tyrell or yourself, my Lord, have the fury to make such a feint convincing. Therefore, Tyrell is the logical choice as I am sure you will want to be at Dry Dock when the city falls."

Lord Dagan steepled his fingers in front of him, remaining silent for a long moment before he spoke again.

"I approve of your plan, Captain Jaeger. Make the preparations you need, and notify me when they are complete."

"Yes, sir," Jaeger bowed to Lord Dagan and left the room.

"The rest of you," Lord Dagan snarled, eying Captain Tyrell. "Lend him whatever help and resources he may need as his status as my Hand dictates. Is that understood?"

"Yes, Lord Dagan!" The others at the table, including Tyrell, chorused. "Long live the great Lord of the seas!"

****

After the meeting of the horde's captains broke up, Lord Dagan returned to his personal chambers. His women were herded from its connecting bedroom as Lord Dagan began the preparations for the work that lay ahead of him. He sealed himself up alone. The heavy metal doors to his chambers were locked and barred against any intrusion.

A pitcher of fresh blood harvested from one of the members of his horde sat atop a table beside which lay an array of strange wands and books wrapped in dried human skin. Lord Dagan took the pitcher of still warm blood and poured a circle as perfectly as he could inside the chamber's walls. When he was done, he sat down cross-legged in the center of the circle. He closed his eyes and pushed the world away, calling the eternal darkness of the void to him.

The electric lights of the room, powered by *The Entropy's* engines, flickered and sparked before going out. The chamber's windows were covered with large, thick sheets of cloth that kept the sunlight of the day outside from entering.

Lord Dagan began to hum deep in his throat, readying himself for the words that needed to be said. He spoke them one by one. They were from a language long lost to mankind. Their sounds were arcane and inhuman. With each word Lord Dagan uttered, the room around him seemed to grow colder.

A bowl of water rested on the floor in front of Lord Dagan. The water inside it stirred, sloshing about with waves that came from nowhere and rippled, increasing in power every second. When the final word was uttered by Lord Dagan, he swept the bowl into his hands, raising it to his lips.

The water burnt with cold and not heat as it was gulped down his throat. Lord Dagan's eyes rolled up inside their sockets to show only white as he entered the world of Great Ones beyond. In this state, in the safety of his circle, Dagan communed with powers that dwarfed anything mankind had ever known. They were amorphous and yet solid. They were dark yet crackled with eldritch energy. Spheres of light danced within Lord Dagan's mind as he and they became one.

The power of the Great Ones flooded his being. He felt them tearing and ripping at his soul. Tentacles laced with jagged barbs raked him, and he relished the pain as his spiritual flesh bled. Lord Dagan wept. Tears slid along the curves of his cheeks. An orgasmic whimper escaped from his tightly closed lips.

In that instant, Lord Dagan was below the waves of the Earth's oceans. He saw the giant sharks called Megalodons swarming, their numbers growing in the depths. He called to them in the name of the Great Ones summoning them, asking them to rise and carry out his will. Countless mouths filled with row upon row of razor-like teeth opened to consume him.

Lord Dagan was thrown into the real world once more as those teeth broke his skin. His scream echoed within the chamber. His body slumped to the floor and lay there as the minutes ticked by.

When he awoke, his body was soaked with sweat. He felt weak and drained, but nonetheless, Lord Dagan smiled. The Megalodons were coming. They would be his servants. The Great Ones had promised it would be so. The Fleet would be smashed by them upon the waves.

****

Captain Stone hit the deck of Dry Dock running as *The Viper's* crew was busy securing the ship. His task force had made it home safely without being forced into an engagement with the Megalodons they had spotted. Stone could have radioed Admiral Campbell to tell him the news while still at sea, but the information he carried was dangerous. He couldn't chance it becoming public before Admiral Campbell knew about it. The crewmembers of the four ships in his task force were sworn to remain silent under penalty of death, but Stone knew that even the sternest punishments and most determined loyal men were human. Eventually, one of them would talk about it to a friend, a wife, a whore; it didn't matter to who. Somehow, the information would leak. It always did.

The Admiral's office was in the center of the city atop the great tower there. Stone picked up his speed, his legs pumping beneath. His breath came in ragged gasps as he ran onward. Veins bulged on his neck and forehead. His heart thundered in his chest and felt as if it were threatening to crack his own ribs from within. He made a mental note to demand that the Admiral order the engineers of Dry Dock to come up with means of fast transport across the surface of the platform that housed the giant city.

He was staggering by the time he reached the hallway leading to the admiral's office. The two armed guards outside the door saw him coming and drew their weapons. Stone came to stop a few feet from the two men and leaned his body against the wall of the hallway as the guards advanced on him. He could hear them demanding he declare his intentions and cast aside any weapons he may be carrying. Their voices sounded distant to his exhausted mind. Still, Stone managed to draw the pistol holstered on his hip slowly and let it drop to clatter on the metal floor at his feet. Then the guards were on him, patting him down from head to toe in search of others. When they found none and backed away, he stared at them, finishing catching his breath.

"My name is Captain Jerod Stone. I was the leader of the task force dispatched to locate the fishing flotilla that went missing recently. I need to see the Admiral at once," Stone told the two guards.

The guards conferred for a moment before they finally moved aside and allowed him access to the door of Admiral Campbell's office. Stone rushed inside. The franticness of his entrance startled Admiral Campbell who had been sorting through some paperwork on his desk.

"Stone?" Campbell looked up at him wide-eyed. "What the Hell?"

"Exactly, sir. Hell, and it's headed our way," Stone said.

"Take a seat, man. You look on the verge of collapse," Campbell ordered.

Stone plopped into the seat across the desk from Campbell.

"Did you locate Jack and the flotilla?"

"They're dead. All dead," Stone frowned.

Campbell spoke up before Stone could say more. "Was it pirates then? The horde is out there somewhere close by. Everything points to them making a run at Dry Dock soon."

Stone shook his head furiously. "It wasn't pirates, Admiral. It was something far worse."

"Worse? What could be worse than a small army of lunatics, rapists, and cannibals at our doorstep?"

"Megalodons, sir. More of them than I have ever seen together before." Stone reached for the pitcher of water on Campbell's desk and one of the glasses near it. Campbell saw him doing so, and gave him a wave, letting Stone know that he should take as much as he needed. Stone poured a glass and chugged it down rapidly, wiping his lips with the back of his hand when he was done. "Sorry, sir," Stone muttered, trying to regain his composure.

"Megalodons?" Campbell asked urging Stone to continue.

"Yes, sir. Dozens and dozens of them. I have never seen anything like it. They weren't just swarming around a sunken ship or murdered whale. They were moving together like a coherent unit. They destroyed Jack's flotilla. There was a single survivor from that massacre, and it *was* a massacre, sir. Those fishing ships didn't have anything more aboard them than small arms to fight off pirates. Those monsters tore the entire flotilla apart."

"Calm down, Captain." Campbell rose from his seat to lean over his desk. "Are you telling me that there's a group of mutated Megalodons out there that is now working together to hunt its prey?"

"Yes, sir, I am," Stone answered firmly. "And they're headed this way. Barring any distractions or bad weather, they could be here as soon as day after tomorrow."

Campbell left Stone sitting in front of his desk and walked to the office's entrance. He poked his head out into the hallway, barking orders at the two guards there. "I want all of the Fleet on condition red immediately, and get Captain Martin to my office ASAP."

The two stunned guards stared at him before he yelled again. "Now damn it!" Campbell raged. He watched as the two guards scampered away to carry out his orders before he returned to his desk.

"Stone, you better be right about this. If not, I swear to you I'll have your head mounted on a pike in the morning."

"I'm right, sir. I wish I weren't, but I saw those things with my own eyes. They're real, and they're coming here," Stone assured the Admiral.

****

Axman and Big Spear walked the streets of the city of Dry Dock. Axman almost passed for a normal citizen of Dry Dock with his dark clothing and pale skin. He had the look of a scholar and would have completely blended in with the throngs of people going about their business around him if not his repeated flipping open and closed the butterfly knife he carried. It was an old habit of his in times of pressure, and he wasn't even fully aware that he doing it until Big Spear caught him by the wrist.

"Put that knife away, man," Big Spear ordered him in a thick voice that resembled the sound of boot heels grinding on gravel. Axman was old enough to remember gravel. His dark hair was speckled with flacks of gray in sharp contrast to the brute beside him. Axman was barely sixteen, but even so he was a giant, standing nearly six foot five. Big Spear's arms were thickly muscled and his chest wide and hard. If Axman nearly blended in, then his companion stuck out like a sore thumb.

It wasn't just Big Spear's size that made him stand out. His hair was spiked into a Mohawk atop his otherwise bald scalp. The smell of the grease that held the spikes in place was foul and emanated from the giant youth like an invisible cloud of pestilence. Flies were drawn to it, and Big Spear swatted a couple of the insects away as Axman closed his knife a final time and buried it in the pocket of his pants.

Big Spear carried himself like the warrior that he was, and his posture and gait drew an occasional extended glance from the crowd of folks on the street with them.

"You need to stop it, too, mate," Axman urged him. "Try to look like an insecure nerd or something okay?"

"What's a nerd?" Big Spear rumbled.

Axman sighed and then punched a fist into Big Spear's shoulder. It was like hitting a brick wall. Axman shook his bruised knuckles in the air as he glared at the young giant.

"Just try to look a little less like a killer and more like someone who lives here. Got it?"

Big Spear nodded, his brow creasing from the thought he gave to Axman's words.

The two of them had come aboard Dry Dock posing as refugees fleeing Lord Dagan's horde. Refugees entering Dry Dock was not an everyday occurrence, but it happened often enough not to raise any eyebrows in suspicion. They were asked a few questions, checked for any weapons deemed too dangerous to be brought onto the station, and then released into the city. The whole thing had gone smoothly just as War Leader Jaeger had told them it would. Technically, Jaeger's rank was captain like all the other leaders of the Horde, but during times when he acted as one of Lord Dagan's hands, one referred to the little man as War Leader or quickly found oneself tied to a post and being flayed.

War Leader Jaeger had sent the two of them aboard Dry Dock to locate explosive materials and place them around the city at critical points. Jaeger apparently already had a contact in the city who would supply them with what they needed. As long as they weren't discovered, it would be a simple job, and one much less risky than being on the ships of the Horde as they came charging in to take the city in the wake of the explosions. Jaeger had told them they would meet their contact in a tavern called The Pentacle of Light.

Axman spotted the tavern up ahead of them on the street and nudged Big Spear. "There it is. Let's get in there and get this job over with."

No one even looked up from their drinks as the two men entered. They made their way to the back and took a table that was off by itself in a dark corner of the establishment's rear. Within minutes of them taking a seat, a gorgeous, big breasted woman approached them.

"I'll have a mug of the strongest spirits you have, wench," Big Spear boomed at the woman.

The woman ignored Big Spear and slid into the booth with them.

"You are from Jaeger, yes?" she asked in a heavily accented voice.

Axman blinked. "You're our contact?"

"Yes," the woman smiled. "Come, we have much to do and little time to do it. Glory awaits us."

Axman and Big Spear exchanged a confused look.

"Do you not understand me?" the woman asked, her cheeks turning red with insult and anger.

"Settle down, lady," Axman said. "We read you loud and clear. We were just . . . just expecting a man, I guess."

The woman snorted. "Women are much more dangerous. Of that, I assure you. Now come. We must go and attend to the things that need to be done before our Lord arrives."

"Lead the way." Axman shrugged and then got to his feet as he and Big Spear followed the woman out of the bar.

Before night fell over the city of Dry Dock, the trio had gathered and placed over thirty charges, and not a single sole had noticed the two refugees and the attractive woman doing anything out of place. The woman, whom Axman learned went by the name of Nyar, knew the ins and outs of Dry Dock well. Their job done, the trio retired to Nyar's residence towards dawn. Axman and Big Spear slept on the floor with dreams of loot and women dancing inside their skulls.

****

The Penelope swung wide, turning her port side to the horizon. Captain Becca Noel sipped at a mug of tea as she sat in her command chair. It was bitter and cold, but it did the job helping her to stay awake. The tea was a blend that was grown on Dry Dock by one of the many farmers that made up its city. This was the first chance Becca had to sample it. It needed something added to its flavor to take the edge off its sharpness but otherwise wasn't all that bad. Patrol duty was as hard on a ship's captain as it was the crew. Every warship in the Fleet, except for Admiral Campbell's flagship, of course, took a turn serving patrol duty. It was a cycling rotation, and *The Penelope's* turn had come up again as it did every two weeks or so.

It was difficult to stay alert and focused when the only things around you were the blue of the ocean and the sky above. After hours and hours of staring at the same scenery, even the threat of the Horde's not to be underestimated fleet of pirate vessels was enough to scare one into staying sharp. Each Patrol run typically last a full day, with the patrol vessel setting out in the morning and heading back as the sunset, then another ship taking its place in the open water.

Becca sat her tea aside and bit at the nail of her right pointer finger in frustration. Part of her desperately wanted something to do, but the rational bits of her brain reminded her that would likely mean a danger to her and her crew.

The Penelope didn't have a lot of the fancy old world tech that many other ships of the Fleet did. Her radio equipment was of the most basic sort and very limited in its range. That same radio equipment also wasn't set up for internal use aboard ship. *The Penelope* didn't have sonar or radar like the larger ships, either. She relied entirely on her lookouts for data gathering about what might be looking out there in the water. What she lacked, though, in terms of that kind of tech, she more than made up for with her *teeth*. *The Penelope* was equipped with twin, surface to surface missile launchers, both forward facing, and a lower placed torpedo launcher on each side of aft hull. In addition, her crew was composed of veterans—men and women who had been plunged into the Hell of combat on the waves and came out of the gaping maw of death alive.

Her EXO, Higdon, entered the ship's small bridge area. "Ma'am, the lookouts are reporting something in the water approaching from the west."

"That's a tad vague, isn't it?" Becca gripped.

"Whatever it is, it's too distant for them to see it clearly even with binoculars, ma'am. I left orders for a runner to be dispatched to the bridge as soon as the identity of the contact or contacts is determined."

Becca sighed. Her ship was meant for combat not patrol duty. She tapped her fingers on the arms of her command chair. "There's not supposed to be anything out there to the west."

"No, ma'am, there's not," Higdon agreed.

"Bring us around on a course for the contact. If it's hostile, I want our launchers pointed in the right direction at least."

Higdon began barking orders to the crew as Becca reached for her tea.

The runner from the bow lookout post came bursting onto the bridge not minutes after the new course had been implemented.

"Megalodons, Captain!" the man shouted at her. "More than I have ever seen!"

Becca's mug fell from her hand, shattering on the floor as she leaped from her seat. "How many?"

"Dozens, Captain," the man panted, trying to catch his breath from his all-out sprint to the bridge.

Higdon stared at the runner as if the man had grown a new head. "That can't right, boy. Megalodons almost never travel together. Surely, you must be wrong."

The runner shook his head violently. "No, sir, I saw them with my own eyes before I was sent to warn you. It's dozens of the things; maybe more."

The Penelope was one tough warship when weighed against other vessels of her size, but the only thing she had aboard that could be used against subsurface targets were her aft torpedo launchers. Even if she had more of the weaponry she needed to fight the beasts, Becca wouldn't have dared stand alone against so many of the monsters.

"Bring us about again on a course for Dry Dock. Engines to full military power!" Becca snapped.

Inwardly, she cringed even as she gave the order. Megalodons were fast, much faster than most ships. If the things opted to come after her ship, she and her crew were going to be in for a fight whether they wanted one or not.

Becca spun on Higdon. "Get to the rear launcher controls. Tell the torpedo crews to open fire, and keep it up the second those sharks come our way. Do not, I repeat, *do not* engage unless they actively alter course to follow us!"

"Aye, Captain," Higdon said and then was gone.

Moments later, Becca heard the aft torpedo launchers open fire. A single volley left the ship for targets she presumed—and hoped—were still far distant.

Unable to be of any effective use from the bridge, Becca ordered the helm to maintain the heading for Dry Dock and rushed to join Higdon at the aft launchers. By the time she had exited the bridge and was running as fast as she could along the side of *The Penelope's* central structure, the launchers had fired twice more, and were now keeping up a steady pace of sending death splashing outward into the waves.

She saw one of the volleys make contact with what must have been a Megalodon a good distance out from the end of the ship. Red water churned and reached for the heavens as the torpedoes detonated. Several more volleys hit their targets as the shockwaves of the blast reached the ship, making it bob upwards. The sudden movement took Becca by surprise and she stumbled, rolling along the deck. Bruised, battered, and cursing, she got to her feet. As she did so, she looked out to port and saw a giant fin cutting through the waves C.B.D.R. (constant bearing, decreasing range) towards her ship.

The shark was coming in too fast for to return to the bridge and order evasive maneuvers, and *The Penelope* had no portside weapons beyond whatever her crew could bring to bear in terms of small arms. Captain Becca Noel gawked at the approaching shark in stark terror as it closed the distance to the ship. Below where Becca stood, the Megalodon plowed into *The Penelope* with enough force to cave the hull inward with a crunching of metal that left her ears ringing. The impact tossed the ship around on the ocean as it took on water. Becca could hear the members of her crew screaming. The aft launcher coughed a final volley of torpedoes into the water before another Megalodon rammed the ship from aft. The giant shark had gotten lucky and somehow must have managed to hit one of the launcher's loading mechanism and magazine because the entire aft section of the ship vanished in a massive explosion. Debris and pieces of the men and women who were assigned to the torpedo crew spiraled through the air over the ship. That explosion triggered another and another that ran the length of *The Penelope,* setting her ablaze from one end to the other. Becca was caught in the blasts, cooked alive where she stood. She didn't even have time to scream before the flames washed over her.

****

War Leader Tyrell stood high atop the central mast of his ship, *The Juggernaut.* The fifteen ships under his command splashed through the waves of the ocean, their engines cranked up to maximum power. Tyrell clutched a battle axe with a blade as wide his chest in one hand and had an AK-47 strapped to his back. His lips were spread in a feral smile that exposed his teeth to the wind. *This was what life was at its fullest,* he thought. *Bearing down on one's enemy, ready to die, but also ready to take as many of the sodding bastards up ahead into the depths with you as you could.*

Fifteen ships were nothing compared to the three dozen vessels of the Fleet that were already noticing their approach and scrambling to get underway and engage them away from the city of Dry Dock. That didn't matter though. Jaeger, the little worm, was counting on Tyrell to bleed them and be bled in turn before making a run for it back out into the open waters.

Some of the ships of his formation were already opening fire on the distant ships defending the city. Missiles whooshed overhead on their way to their targets. Wide bore cannons thundered. Torpedoes raced across the waves ahead of his vessels.

Tyrell whooped, waving his axe above his head as he watched one of the vessels of the Fleet take a direct hit in its center. Flames blossomed and spread along its deck. He imagined the glorious sound of its crew howling in fear and agony as they dove overboard to avoid being fried where they stood. He enjoyed a few more moments of such glory before the Fleet got its act together enough to begin returning fire.

"Incoming!" he heard of one *The Juggernaut's* crew yelling below him. Tyrell glanced skyward to behold a tomahawk cruise missile as it streaked over his ship. The missile overshot his flagship but caught *The Reaper* behind her directly in its bow. *The Reaper* jerked on the waves as if the hand of God himself had reached down to stop her forward movement. Her aft section skewed sideways bringing her port side around towards ships of the Fleet ahead.

Tyrell could see that *The Reaper* was crippled and taking on water. Even so, he smiled as he watched her crew staying at their posts and unloading the portside mass of cannons at the Fleet. He wanted very badly to ignore Jaeger's plan and charge headlong the rest of the way into and among the ships of the Fleet. The Horde and its ships were designed for close in combat, not this long range tossing of stones at one another. He wanted to leap onto the deck of the Fleet vessel and feel the blood its crew spraying onto his face and arms as he hacked into them with his battle axe. He couldn't though. Lord Dagan would skin him alive in front of his crew if didn't follow Jaeger's plan.

He snagged up his radio and shouted orders into it to the other captains of the Horde. "Give them another taste Hell boys and then disengage. Follow *The Juggernaut's* lead for course and speed!"

Fire rained from the sky on the ships of the Horde and the Fleet alike as the two groups continued to hammer at one another with everything they had. Tyrell felt a pang of heartbreak as at last *The Juggernaut* veered away from the ships of the Fleet. He unswung his AK-47 from his back and raised it towards his enemies. He knew he was too distant to hit anything barring a miracle, but opening up with the rifle on full auto made him feel better anyway.

The ships under Tyrell's command were now in full retreat. A good number of Admiral Campbell's ships of the Fleet were pursuing them just as Jaeger had predicted they would. Tyrell leaned over the side of the mast and shouted down for his crew to maintain *The Juggernaut's* best possible speed for as long as the ship could take it. Jaeger's plan called for him to draw away as many ships of the Fleet as he could but said nothing about what to do after that was accomplished. The Horde task force under his command had only lost three ships in their charge. The Fleet had lost five thanks mostly to the Horde's insane ferocity and the element of surprise. Admiral Campbell, or whoever was leading the ships of the Fleet, had only sent twenty after him. To Tyrell, that was enough of an equalizer to call the next battle a fair fight. He knew it would happen, too, as soon as they were far enough from Dry Dock.

****

Admiral Campbell was just receiving his first word of the all-out attack by The Horde on his ships surrounding Dry Dock when the unthinkable happened. Explosions rang out, lighting the night sky all over the giant platform city. He watched, stunned and horrified, through the window of his office as the city of Dry Dock was being torn apart before his eyes.

The surprise attack by the Horde using the cover of night to slip into combat range with the ships of the Fleet was a tactic he had been ready for, even expecting to happen. Whatever was happening in the city itself was a whole other matter entirely. As he continued to watch the destruction unfolding before him, he realized he should have seen it coming too. Never until recently, though, had he needed to worry so much about members of the Horde coming *on board and* unseen to wreck their havoc. That had to be what had happened. There was no other explanation his mind could come up with. Somehow, members of the Horde, likely posing as traders or refugees, had snuck onto the Dry Dock and planted charges throughout her. He should have increased the giant platform city's security as soon as he had taken command of it. He knew this now, but it was too late. The damage was done, and the people of Dry Dock were paying the price for his shortsightedness. The worst part of the explosions was that they were centered mainly in the living areas of the platform city. The handful that weren't targeted the city's defense emplacements. None of the city's farming structures and green house, machine shops, or storage depots had been targeted. Admiral Campbell knew that Lord Dagan wanted those intact for when he emerged victorious in this battle. The amount of food, fuel, and ammo just currently stored away in the city would buy the Horde long, comfortable months of not having to scavenge for their needs. If Lord Dagan were smart—and Campbell knew he was—he'd take up permanent residence here. Dry Dock was as close to being completely self-sustaining as anything that remained in this nightmare of a world.

Captain Martin still stood at the table where she and Campbell had been busy preparing to confront the Megalodon threat that was quickly approaching the station as well. They had received numerous further reports from other ships on patrol in the sector where the giant beasts had been spotted. The Megalodons were very much still in route to Dry Dock. They, not the Horde, were the focus of his attention and Martin's before the attack had begun. A map of the ocean sectors around the city laid rolled open on the table in front of Martin. Her hands had clenched upon it, tearing the precious paper in her grip as her tightened fingers became fists. Campbell saw that she was just as shocked and angry as he was.

Martin's new ship, *The 2112,* was still docked to the city and not part of the battle raging on the waves. It had escaped being damaged by both the Horde's attack and the onboard saboteurs. Campbell could see it from where he stood at the high vantage point of his office's open window.

"Get to your ship!" he ordered Martin. "Too much of the Fleet has broken away from the station in pursuit of the Horde ships. There's no way in cold Hell that was all of them unless something really bad happened to Lord Dagan's people since the last time we went face to face."

Martin nodded, snapping out of her frozen state.

"Take command of everything we've got left around the station. Call back the ships that left if you can, but above all, be ready for Hell. Those Megalodons can't be too far off and neither can the rest of the Horde."

Martin started to leave and stopped in her tracks. "Aren't you coming, sir?"

Campbell shook his head. "No. As much as I would like to . . . no. My responsibility is to help the people of this city. We need to find whoever set those charges that just ripped it a new one before they can do any more damage."

"Understood," Martin said then saluted him. "I won't let you down out there, sir."

"See that you don't," Campbell snapped despite himself. "We can't afford to lose this one, Captain Martin."

****

Lord Dagan stood on the bridge of *The Entropy*. The bridge was a sharp contrast to most bridges of post-flood vessels. Large flat screen monitors lined its forward section. Four of the screens showed images of what lay to each side of the massive ship. One of the others was lit up with a real time tactical image of the Horde's vessels in formation around it. Two others were tasked to radar and sonar readings respectively. The sheer amount of information available so readily before him often gave Lord Dagan an edge over any group of ships stupid enough to challenge his Horde.

Banger, his weapons and radar officer, sat at his station cracking his knuckles impatiently and waiting for the action to start. Shelia, his comm officer, wore a rather out of place chainmail bikini that left little to the imagination, looked worried, her eyes glued to the screens. Flyboy, the only other person on the bridge, sat at the joint helm/engineering console. His fingers danced over the keyboard in front of him making course changes as needed to keep *The Entropy* dead center in the Horde's advancing formation. All of them were veterans, the best of the best that Horde had to offer or they wouldn't have been aboard *The Entropy* at all.

"My Lord," Banger called out from his position behind where Lord Dagan stood. "We've got contacts closing fast. C.B.D.R."

Without turning to look at Banger, Lord Dagan spoke. "Contacts? From where? There's no way the Fleet could know we're coming yet."

"The contacts are closing on the rear of the Fleet, my Lord. They are subsurface and moving at speeds far too fast to be anything the Fleet could throw at us," Banger answered.

"Subsurface?" Lord Dagan half snarled. "How many?"

Banger called up a sonar image on one of the main screens for Lord Dagan to see. "Their formation is too tight at the speed they are moving for me to get a detailed read on their numbers. I would wager over two dozen though."

Lord Dagan allowed himself a wicked grin.

Shelia saw it and asked, "My Lord, do you know what they are?"

Lord Dagan nodded proudly. "The Great Ones have heard my incantations child. Those contacts are their children coming to our aid."

"You're saying they're biologics?" Banger asked, risking Dagan's wrath for speaking out of place. He quickly added, "That would make sense, my Lord. The only things in the oceans I know of that big and that can move that fast are Megalodons."

"Yes, Megalodons," Lord Dagan laughed. It was a sound full of cruelty and perverted joy. "They come!"

Raising the black trident he held towards the bridge's ceiling, he shook it violently. "A reckoning is at hand for Admiral Campbell and his poor pathetic Fleet!"

"My Lord!" Banger spoke up again. "The approaching contacts aren't slowing to join the Horde's formation."

"Why should they?" Lord Dagan whirled on Banger. "They are the children of the very waves themselves! If they wish to go ahead of us to draw first blood from the Fleet, it is their right to so."

"No, my Lord," Banger said carefully, "You fail to understand me. The contacts aren't passing us. They are coming in on collision courses with our rear most vessels!"

"What?" Lord Dagan shrieked. "Why would they do that?"

Banger cringed as he spoke. "I don't know, my Lord, but they are."

"Your instruments are wrong, boy! The Megalodons have been sent to aid us!"

"Look at the screen, my Lord!" Banger said pointing at the one featuring a radar-based, real time display of the Horde's formation.

Upon it, over two dozen massive red blips were closing fast on the blue blips which represented the vessels of the Horde. Lord Dagan watched in disbelief as the fastest of the red blips reached their targets and rammed into them.

Shelia's comm station erupted with a flood of incoming distress calls and requests for orders.

"Lord Dagan," she informed him, "several Horde ships have taken damage and are requesting permission to break formation to engage the hostiles."

Lord Dagan ripped his metal, tentacle covered helmet from his head and flung it at the closest screen. The screen shattered in a shower of sparks as the helmet struck it.

"The Great Ones have betrayed us!" Lord Dagan raged, spittle flying from his lips, as his hands yanked clumps of his own hair from his scalp.

"What do we do, my Lord?" Flyboy shouted.

"Do I have permission to open fire on the hostile contacts?" Banger wailed.

"Evasive action!" Lord Dagan bellowed. "Engage contacts at will, and have the other ships do the same!"

The Horde's formation broke apart as the ships comprising it all changed course individually in their panic as the Megalodons continued to move through them, striking at any given opportunity. *The Skull,* one of the Horde's destroyers, turned too hard to port and collided with *The Rapture.* *The Rapture* was a small yacht that been retrofitted into an attack craft. Its hull gave way as *The Skull* smashed into it. Loaded down with munitions for the coming battle with the Fleet, *The Rapture* exploded into a growing ball of fire whose flames reached upwards towards the heavens. The collision didn't leave *The Skull* undamaged. The shrapnel from *The Rapture* fell upon its decks, and soon *The Skull,* too, was ablaze.

Many ships of the Horde were firing wildly at the Megalodons with whatever they had onboard and could bring to bear on the giant sharks. The bulk of the panicked fire missed its targets, but given their close proximity, didn't fail to hit other ships of the Horde.

Lord Dagan howled like a wounded wolf as he watched his own ships tearing themselves apart. Some idiot aboard one of the Horde ships closest to *The Entropy* launched a surface to surface missile in the direction of a Megalodon as it sped passed her along her starboard side. The missile detonated as it hit *The Entropy's* near her bridge. The shockwave of the blast sent Lord Dagan staggering. Banger and Shelia held onto their stations for dear life until it passed. Flyboy was so busy trying to keep *The Entropy* from overrunning the Horde vessels surrounding her that he didn't even seem to notice the blast.

"My Lord . . .!" Shelia started but never got the chance to finish.

"Silence!" Lord Dagan shouted in a voice like thunder as he reared his arm back and threw his trident into Shelia. Its three, sharpened prongs impaled her, the center one piercing her heart. Blood bubbled up inside Shelia's still open mouth as she toppled backwards and fell once more into her seat at the comm station. Her eyes were wide as her hands clutched the shaft of the trident behind the prongs that buried in her flesh. She gave the trident a weak tug, attempting to pull it out of her, and then died, slumping sideways in her chair.

"Get us out of here!" Lord Dagan ordered Flyboy as he rushed to lean onto the helm station beside where Flyboy sat.

"I'm trying, sir!" Flyboy pleaded. The tone of his voice left no doubt that Flyboy thought he would be the next member of the bridge crew to die at Lord Dagan's hand.

"Bring us about hard!" Lord Dagan rasped.

"But, sir, *The Zombie* is in our path!" Flyboy argued.

"It's a frigate!" Lord Dagan boomed. "Go through her, damn you!"

Flyboy did as he was told. *The Entropy* came to bear on *The Zombie* and literally smashed the smaller vessel to bits as she plowed through her in an attempt to leave the chaotic combat zone the Horde's formation had become.

A Megalodon made a run at *The Entropy*. Banger saw the monster coming and did his best to stop it, targeting the giant shark with a volley of hastily fired torpedoes. They struck the shark head on and must have wounded the creature badly. It veered away from *The Entropy* in the wake of the torpedoes' explosions. It didn't matter though. Two more Megalodons took its place and impacted with *The Entropy* at ramming speed. The collision was so powerful that *The Entropy* rolled in water.

Banger was screaming at the top of his lungs as *The Entropy* overturned in the water and began to sink. Entire sections of her port hull were simply gone, and her topside decks were below the waves at a sideways angle. Water came rushing onto the bridge, making contact with strands of damaged electrical cables that had collapsed from the bridge's ceiling.

The invincible Lord Dagan met death, not from the waves, but from the currents of energy that shook his body where he stood knee deep in water as he rose to his feet on one of the overturned bridge's walls. Foam flew from his lips, his eyes rolled upwards as he body danced and jerked about while he was cooked alive from the inside.

****

Captain Martin managed to get aboard *The 2112* and assume command of the portion of the Fleet still surrounding Dry Dock just in time to get organized enough to meet Lord Dagan's Horde should it decide to show itself. She knew the Admiral was right in guessing that the small number of Horde vessels who had attacked the Fleet and broke off, heading away from Dry Dock, couldn't be all that Lord Dagan had to throw at them. The surprise attack and the explosions on the platform city itself had to be distractions, though seriously hurtful ones, to keep their attention away from whatever might be coming at them next.

She redeployed the remaining Fleet vessels into a looser formation and ordered them away from Dry Dock into a position she hoped would allow her to meet Lord Dagan's Horde, regardless of which direction it appeared from, before it reached the city.

Martin was a warrior and a leader, second only to Admiral Campbell himself among the captains of the Fleet in terms of her prowess and skill at dealing out death. Right now, she doubted herself though. How could she not with so much at stake? If Dry Dock fell to the Horde, not only would thousands of people die—or worse find themselves slaves under the reign of the demented and madness driven Lord Dagan, but the Fleet would be in no shape to retake it. Lord Dagan and his Horde had always been the Fleet's betters when it came to close in combat of the hand to hand nature. The Horde was composed of bloodthirsty lunatics who thrived on feeling the flesh of their enemies give way to the swings of their swords, axes, and clubs. The sailors of the Fleet were professional men and women, yes, but they weren't animals. In fights like the ones the Horde thrived on, they just didn't have the suicidal and berserker rage filled fury of the Horde. That meant Martin had to stop the Horde here and now before they ever set foot aboard the station.

She had to consider the Megalodon threat as well. While the great beasts couldn't hope to savage Dry Dock itself, they could tear whatever remained of the Fleet apart easily if she weren't careful in how she approached dealing with them. In essence, Martin found herself forced into preparing for a war on two fronts without any idea on which side it would start.

"Gary," she called the name of *The 2112's* radar/sonar tech softly. "What do you have for me?"

"Actually, ma'am, I might have some good news for you. There's a large cluster of contacts spread out to the northwest, and they're acting rather erratically. There were two large groups of contacts at first, but when they met up . . . well, it's like they appear to have engaged each other," Gary answered.

"Tell me more," Martin urged Gary, taking her seat in *The 2112's* captain chair.

"Not much more to tell, ma'am. The two groups of contacts are now one and appear to be in battle based on the speed and nature of their maneuvers. If you really want to know what's going on out there, Dry Dock has two helos aboard it, ma'am. If they survived the explosions that swept the city, you could order one out for a more detailed look. I know both helos are decked out with top of the line comm gear."

Martin smiled. "Good thinking, Gary. Get in touch with whoever you can aboard Dry Dock, and get one those birds in the air A.S.A.P."

"Yes, ma'am," Gary nodded.

"And those are the only contacts detected within our extended sensor range?" Martin asked.

Gary's head bobbed up and down again as he worked on raising someone on Dry Dock to pass on her order regarding the helo.

"Have all other Fleet vessels form up on us. I want us all spread out like a wall of ships between the group of contacts and the city."

As the helmsman cranked up the power to *The 2112's* engines and changed her heading, Martin activated the ship's internal comm. "All hands, Condition Red. Report to battle stations."

****

Eric ran through his preflight as fast as he could, which wasn't as fast as he would have liked. The Seawolf was old, really old. It wasn't a true Seawolf, either, though he had given it that name. The bird had been mostly cobbled together from the pieces of too many other helos than he liked to think about. It passed the safety checks of Dry Dock's engineers, though, or he wouldn't have dared take it up. Despite his anxiety today, he had flown the Seawolf numerous times before on recon ops that the higher ups in Dry Dock hierarchy had ordered. Today was different though. A good portion of the city of Dry Dock was in flames. Before he got her blades moving above him, he could hear the distant cries and shouts of the city's populace even from the elevated area of the helipad. He supposed those cries were what was really bothering him. He hadn't been able to locate his wife before he had been handed orders to get in the air and could only pray she and their three-year-old son were okay. Eric wanted to be out in the city searching for them and doing what he could to help all those who were injured in the blasts or left homeless with nothing in the world but the clothes on their backs. He finished his preflight just as his co-pilot, Warren, climbed into the bird and took the seat next to him.

"It's a mess out there," Warren told him. Somehow the words seemed so much of an understatement they almost rang with an edge of insult to what the city of Dry Dock was going through. Eric glared at him, but Warren just shrugged.

"Our orders are to head out and get a look at what's going on at the coordinates Captain Martin of *The 2112* sent us."

Warren looked over the scrap of paper containing the hastily written orders on it as Eric handed it to him. "Wait. Isn't this where the ships of the Horde are supposed to be?"

Eric nodded. "Yep. This could very well be our first combat run."

The two helos owned by the city of Dry Dock were such precious items that the city never dared risk them in combat. Both birds were armed with duel rocket launcher tubes on their sides, but since the helos had been built the weapons had never been fired in anything beyond tests. For this Captain Martin, whoever she was, to be able to order them into the air on such short notice *and* into a possible combat zone, the level of power she held must be staggering. Eric knew she was part of the Fleet, and that the city and the Fleet were now one and the same. The two had given up being allies and merged completely with Governor Bachman's passing. From what he had heard, though, some guy named Campbell who went by the rank of Admiral was supposed to be in charge, not some lady captain. Orders were orders, though, and there was no doubt that these were official ones.

"We're just supposed to do a flyby and see what's going on, right?" Warren did his best to fake a brave laugh. "Nobody said we have to get too close to the area, if you know what I mean."

"Going up," Eric said, ignoring Warren. The Seawolf lifted from the helipad and rose into the darkness of the night sky. It flew over the wall of the ships the Fleet had lined itself up into in front of Dry Dock. Warren gave them a wave as Eric focused on getting them where they needed to go.

The flight was a short one. Eric had made it that way by pouring on all the speed the Seawolf could muster. He wanted this op over with as fast as possible, not just because of what it entailed, but so he could get back aboard Dry Dock and go searching for his family.

"Holy crap," Eric heard Warren mutter as they came into view of the designated area they were supposed to check out. It looked like a war zone because it was one. The battle appeared to be over, but the broken, blazing hulls of numerous ships floated on the ocean's surface below them.

"Guess we don't have to worry about getting shot at after all," Warren said.

"Bringing us in for a closer look," Eric informed him.

The Seawolf buzzed past the decimated area and swung around to come in just above the burning wreckage that had once been the ships of the Horde. Eric wondered what could have taken out so many ships.

"Hey," Warren nudged him. "What's that down there moving in the water?"

Eric hoped it wasn't survivors. They didn't have the space or fuel to take people onboard the Seawolf. She just wasn't built for that sort of thing like her name sake had been in the old world. Aside from that, if there were survivors, they would be members of the Horde. Everyone, Eric included, had heard enough stories about Lord Dagan and his men to know that some of them were cannibals, and all of them were stark, raving mad. It would be a cold day in Hell before Eric helped one of those bastards, but he had no desire to hang out in the air above the scene of the battle and watch them drown either.

Squinting with his eyes, Eric strained to see what Warren was pointing at. When he did, he recognized it at once. He could tell it was the very upmost top of a giant fin. It sped through the water in the direction of the helo.

"Take us up, man!" Warren was shouting. "Take us up now!"

Eric pulled back on the helo's throttle, and the bird shot upwards in the sky just as a Megalodon fully broke the surface of the water. It leaped into the air, its mouth open wide, passing through the space where the Seawolf had been only seconds before.

"Holy!" Eric shouted himself. "That was too bloody close, mate!"

"You're telling me?" Warren snapped at him.

When the helo was well above the distance Eric thought a Megalodon might be able to jump, he leveled the bird out and came around to take another look at the scene of the battle below. Warren's attention had never left the water below.

"There's more than one of those things," Warren told him. "I'm counting over a dozen fins moving about down there. I would wager there are a lot more that we can't see too."

Warren shook his head. Eric wasn't sure if it was in disgust or relief.

"Those things really tore the Horde a new one, didn't they? Look at that mess. I mean, that's got to be close to everything the Horde had. It has to be."

"We better start calling this in," Eric said, watching the sharks moving about in the water underneath the Seawolf. The giant beasts almost looked as if they were forming up like naval vessels getting ready for another battle.

Eric listened to Warren hailing *The 2112* on the Helo's radio and reporting what they had discovered as he watched the giant sharks, as one, pick a new heading and go swimming away from the wreckage of the Horde ships. Eric didn't have to double check their bearing to know that the beasts were on a direct course for the city of Dry Dock.

****

Admiral Campbell didn't like leaving the defense of Dry Dock to Captain Martin. He hated it. He knew, though, that of all the captains of the Fleet she was the best qualified. Martin was a warrior through and through. She might not have his years of experience, but she had keen instincts and a sharp mind. Campbell was almost jealous of her. While she was out there doing his job, he was stuck on Dry Dock trying to handle a whole other matter of chaos. The explosive charges that members of the Horde had set when they had come aboard pretending to be refugees had killed over two hundred of the city's populace while wounding a great many more. Just as bad, many folks were now essentially homeless. The members of the Horde had primarily targeted the living section of the city with their cowardly attack.

All the citizens of Dry Dock were Campbell's responsibility now. He had given his word to Bachman that he would watch over them and protect the city. No matter how much others told him it wasn't his fault, he knew it was. If he had just been more focused, thought things through better, maybe he would have thought to increase the city's security given that he had known the ships of the Horde wee nearby, and that Lord Dagan was planning on making an attempt at taking Dry Dock. Beating himself up was pointless. That's why he had delegated command of the Fleet to Martin. Campbell swore to himself that he would locate the members of the Horde that did this to the city, his city, and make them pay.

Kelvin Goh was the chief of Dry Dock's security under Governor Bachman, and it was to him that Campbell turned for help. He had known the man for years, though never closely, and respected Goh. Goh had retired from his post with Bachman's death, waiting perhaps to see if Campbell was going to reinstate him, or choose a new head of security of his own. Much to his shame, Campbell hadn't done either during his first week as Dry Dock's new leader. Campbell had left security matters to the personnel from the Fleet who had come aboard the station with him, assuming that as experienced as his sailors were, they could figure out how to deal with things in the city. The terror that had struck Dry Dock proved they weren't ready for such wildly new duties—especially without direction from him—any more than he was fully prepared to take over as governor.

Campbell found Goh out in the streets working hard to help those hurt in the unexpected terror attack. If Goh blamed him for it, the thin, agile man had too much honor to show it. He greeted Campbell as if nothing had happened and offered his services in whatever manner Campbell needed.

Having sent away all of his personal guards to either help with the chaos within in the city or to aid Martin aboard the ships of the Fleet should the rest of the Horde show itself, Campbell asked Goh to be his guard and guide as the two of them set about their search for the members of the Horde that had done this horrible thing to Dry Dock.

Goh knew the city like it was a part of his body. It didn't take the two of them long to take down the Horde members posing as refugees. He and Campbell tracked them to a set of quarters not far from the platform's southern edge in a more rundown portion of the city. They stood outside those quarters now, preparing to make their move.

"I have heard much about the woman who lives here. She is called Serena by some. However, I very much doubt that is her real name," Goh told Campbell. "She came aboard a little over a month ago and has kept to herself during that time. I had her pegged as trouble, but she was cunning enough to never give me a real reason to come down hard on her. I might have done so anyway, but around the time I was considering it, the seriousness of Governor Bachman's illness became public. In matters such as these, one must often weigh the gain against the loss. At the time, I suppose I felt that I would lose more trust from the citizens of the Dry Dock for acting without proper cause than there was to be gained by raiding her home."

Campbell saw that Goh was blaming himself as well. "You didn't do this, Goh. This wasn't your fault."

Goh shrugged. "Did you bring a weapon, Admiral? I fear these men we seek are of a very dangerous type."

Campbell drew a Glock from the shoulder holster he wore underneath the jacket of his uniform.

Goh whistled at the sight of it. "That is one fine pistol, sir."

"It will do the job. That's all that matters." Campbell dismissed the compliment. "Do you have a weapon?"

Goh laughed, though there was no smugness in his voice as he answered, "I am the only weapon I need, Admiral."

"Let's get this over with then," Campbell said, and approached the door to Serena's quarters.

It was flung open in front of them as Serena and two men came bursting out at them. Serena made a beeline for Goh. She gave a feral shriek as she leaped through the air towards him. Campbell watched Goh easily block her flying kick, but she landed well, and went at him again with a flurry of strikes almost too fast for Campbell's eyes to follow.

Campbell cursed himself for allowing himself to be focused on Goh's fight when he had one of his own at hand. One of the two men who followed Serena out was more of a mountain than a man. His hair was spiked atop his scalp, and tattoos covered every inch of his exposed skin. A nose ring, like something one would have imagined seeing on a bull, dangled from his nostrils. The giant plowed into Campbell before he could aim his weapon and shout for the two men to stop. Campbell's Glock went flying from his grasp to clatter along the metal of Dry Dock, sliding far beyond his reach.

The impact of the giant ramming into him knocked the breath from Campbell's lungs as the giant picked him up effortlessly and slammed Campbell into the wall of another set of quarters behind him. Campbell's head was flung back, hitting the wall hard, even as his back made contact with it. His vision blurred, and pain flared throughout his body, but Campbell shook it off. Balling his hands into fists, he raised them and brought them down on to the shoulders of the giant with all the strength he could manage. The giant grunted, but his hold on Campbell remained firm. Campbell looked down from where the giant mashed him against the wall and looked into the giant's eyes. One of the giant's pupils was black; the other green. His teeth were bared in an animal-like snarl as he reared his head back and slammed his own forehead into

Campbell's chest. Campbell heard the pop of at least one of his ribs giving way under the force of the blow. The sound and pain made him vomit. Doing so likely saved his life. The giant released him and retreated a few steps, wiping at the half digested puke covering his face and arms.

Campbell recovered quickly and took a swing at the giant. His right fist met the giant's jaw, and while the giant staggered, it was Campbell who cried out in pain. His knuckles felt broken, and hitting the giant had been like hitting a brick wall. Campbell knew he couldn't let up, though, or the giant would have him again. His foot lashed out making contact with the giant's groin. The giant whelped and collapsed forward onto his knees. Campbell was about to hit him again, hoping to finish him, when something plunged into his side. He looked down to see the hilt of a butterfly knife protruding from him. Its blade was buried in his guts. A little man dressed in dark clothes wearing nerdy glasses was sneering at him as he twisted the blade deeper. The little man jerked the blade free of Campbell, further opening the gash in the admiral's side.

The world spun around Campbell as he met the deck of Dry Dock face-first with the snapping sound of breaking bone. The weight of his own body had broken his nose. Campbell lifted his head, spitting teeth and blood as he tried to stand. A large, heavy foot was placed on his already bruised back, shoving him back down.

The little man was cackling like a deranged girl who had just found a dead squirrel to play with.

"Stay down!" the giant's voice boomed like thunder.

Then Goh was there. The thin security chief moved like lightning. He had taken the small man with the butterfly knife from behind, breaking his neck with a quick fluid jerk before either of the members of the Horde had time to react.

The giant watched his friend's corpse slump to rest where Goh's feet had been. Goh was still moving though. The tip of his boot connected with the underside of the giant's chin. Campbell heard the giant's teeth crushing each other inside his unexpectedly and forcefully closed mouth. The giant managed to take a swing at Goh, but the security chief blocked it, diving closer to the big man. Goh's fist whipped out, bashing in the giant's throat. The giant's skin turned blue as he struggled to breathe and couldn't. Campbell knew his windpipe must have been crushed from Goh's strike. Goh wasn't done yet though. He swung around where he stood, smashing his fist into the giant's forehead. The giant fell over and lay still.

"Admiral!" Goh shouted, moving to Campbell's side. "Are you okay?"

Campbell nodded. "Thanks to you."

Goh helped Campbell to his feet.

"The woman?" Campbell asked.

"Dead," Goh said, and grinned. "I am sorry to say that she wouldn't consider surrendering."

Campbell took in the sight of the two dead members of the Horde in front of where he and Goh stood.

"Goh," Campbell said. "If you want your old job back, it's yours. You never should have retired."

Goh bowed to Campbell. "I shall accept that offer, sir. It appears you are going to need me much more than Governor Bachman ever did."

****

Captain Martin didn't know whether to feel relieved or scared out of her mind when the news came in. The Helo she had dispatched on a recon run to check out what was happening to the North reported that the Horde fleet had been destroyed by the Megalodon pack headed toward Dry Dock.

The bridge crew of *The 2112* was cheering around her. Their cries of glee echoed off the walls of the bridge. Some of them had actually left their posts and were outright dancing. The destruction of the Horde was indeed a great victory and one the Fleet had never been able to accomplish on its own. Martin knew, though, that the same pack of Megalodons that had just slain the Fleet's worst enemies would be bearing down on them soon enough. Too soon.

"Quiet!" Martin shouted. The celebration around her stopped at once as her crew came to attention waiting to hear what she had to say.

"Gary!" Martin snapped. "Status of northward contacts!"

Gary scurried to his station as the other members of the crew retook theirs as well. He plopped into the chair in front of the console and went to work. "Sub-surface contacts are lesser in number, captain, but they are headed this way." Gary's skin went white as he added, "ETA in ten minutes."

"You heard the man, folks," Captain Martin told the bridge crew. "The Horde may be gone—and while that's a wonderful thing that I am sure none of us thought we would see in our lifetimes given the state of this world, our day isn't over yet. A herd of giant sharks, the likes of which no one has ever encountered before, is on its way here . . . to us. "

Martin paused, allowing her words to sink in before she continued. "Gary, how many contacts remain?"

Gary coughed, struggling to speak, before he got his answer out. "My screen is showing eighteen, Captain."

"Eighteen," Martin repeated the number. "Eighteen, folks. We've lost all contact with the detachment of the Fleet that broke away in pursuit of the ships of the Horde who made a run at Dry Dock earlier today. I think it's best to assume that both they and the ships they were after are also destroyed. The twenty-three vessels we have left, right here, right now, are all that remains of the Fleet. Those giant monsters on their way to us just eliminated an equal or larger sized fleet of Horde ships with minimal losses to their own numbers. As much as we may want to celebrate the destruction of the Horde, we're trouble ladies and gentlemen . . . Big trouble."

The faces of the crewmen surrounding her had lost their joy. Each and every one of them heard what she had said and knew it was true. Often it took more than a single ship to go head to head with a Megalodon and the herd of sharks approaching them nearly equaled the Fleet's numbers.

Captain Martin snapped her fingers. "Patch me through to the rest of the Fleet," she ordered. "All hands, maintain Condition Red. A herd of Megalodons is fast closing on our position, and it's up to us to show those monsters that we humans have teeth too!"

****

The ships of the Fleet were still deployed in a long line resembling a wall in front of the city of Dry Dock waiting on the herd of Megalodons to arrive. Captain Martin stood behind Gary at the sonar station. Her attention was completely focused there as she watched for any sign of the great beasts. She was not alone in her action. Every captain in the

Fleet with a ship that had sonar capability was likely doing the same thing. There were lookouts posted on the masts, towers, and bows of every ship, as well straining their eyes for the herd's approach.

The sonar screen lit up as the herd came into view. There were close to two dozen Megalodons, all moving fast and closing on the Fleet from the North. Martin felt anger as she saw the images of the giant sharks. Mankind had endured so much since the floods, and now the last great center of humanity was being threatened by animals that had no right to even exist.

"Patch me through to the Fleet," Martin ordered.

Her comm officer gave her the signal that she was on.

"All ships pick your targets and fire at will. We have to stop these things here and now. We won't be getting a second chance."

The night lit up as the ships of the Fleet opened fire at the approaching Megalodons. Torpedoes launched, splashing into the water, charging forward at their targets. Missile shot skywards, only to arc downwards and plunge into the waves. Heavy machine guns on decks chattered, spitting spent shell casings as tracer rounds burnt orange and red amid the barrage of death they spewed. Captain Martin watched the Hell that was being unleashed and hoped it would be enough. It wasn't.

The Megalodons took some losses before they reached the line of the ships in front of Dry Dock. The fastest of the Megalodons met the bulk of the inbound torpedoes head on. One after another they struck the giant shark, blasting massive holes into its body. Blood, teeth, and flesh flowed away from it as it raged beneath the waves. Another Megalodon, one of the smaller of the creatures, was gutted by a torpedo. It continued on through the water, leaking red and dragging long strands of its own innards behind it before it finally stopped moving and rolled over, floating upwards. Another took a direct strike from a missile and was blown to bits of pulp that sprayed towards the heavens in the ensuing explosion.

In all, twelve Megalodons died or were too wounded to continue the fight before the herd of the creatures reached the Fleet's lines. Unfortunately, that left still left enough of the Megalodons to do some serious damage as they struck.

A Megalodon ripped through the under hull of *The Holmes* as if the metal were wet paper. The ship broke apart in its wake. Men and women dived into the water trying to escape the explosion that was sure to come with the damage done to the ship's engine. A second Megalodon swooped in, making a meal of most of them. Its wide open mouth took them in.

The Enterprise fared little better. The largest of the Megalodons went after it. *The Enterprise* was a full out battleship. In another time and place no shark could have ever hurt it, but this was a new world with a new breed of shark. The Megalodon that rammed it was as large as the ship itself. The giant shark came partially out of the water, leaping against the *The Enterprise's* starboard side. Metal screamed and folded inward as the battleship rolled over into the waves. It took only seconds for the Megalodon to double back, building up speed as it came, to finish the ship, and make sure it sunk.

Captain Martin watched *The Rain* pushing its engines beyond the redline in an attempt to avoid the Megalodon charging it. *The Rain* was a frigate, small and fragile looking compared to the monster it was engaged with. The frigate disintegrated before Martin's eyes as the Megalodon caught the small vessel and made contact with it. The destruction of the frigate didn't even slow the giant shark down. It simply changed course, keeping its speed, to crash into the portside of *The Jones*. The crew of *The Jones* had no time to dodge or even brace for the monster's impact because it came so suddenly. The Megalodon went through *The Jones,* emerging from the rupture it made in the ship's hull. The shark didn't escape unbloodied. *The Jones* was a heavily armored ship and the jaggedness of its broken hull left the Megalodon leaving a trail of red as it sped away from the sinking ship.

The only other frigate left in the Fleet was *The Atom Smasher.* It made no attempt to run from the Megalodon inbound on its portside. Its crew lined that side of its deck, peppering the approaching monster with small arms fire. It was a tactic Martin knew was useless. Handheld weapons couldn't possibly do more than make the giant shark angrier than it already was. Martin knew at once what the captain of *The Atom Smasher* was planning. She wanted with all her soul to be able to call out to the ship and order them not to do it. Martin saw the Megalodon ram into the hull of *The Atom Smasher.* At that moment, the captain of the little frigate must have hit the activation mechanism for whatever detonator he and his crew had rigged up. The frigate blossomed into a ball of fire and exploding shrapnel that consumed the Megalodon as the ship broke apart in a hellish fury.

The Diana didn't go down without a fight. The ship's CIWS targeted the Megalodon approaching it and opened up at the creature with a virtual wall of bullets. The high powered rounds the CIWS spat splashed beneath the waves to blow chunks of flesh from the giant shark's form and left the creature's body riddled with gaping wounds. The shark was dead before it struck *The Diana* but its impact still caused the ship to lurch sideways on the waves, her hull cracked and taking on water.

Finally, it was *The 2112's* turn to face the oncoming herd of death. Captain Martin stood in front of her command chair. Her bridge crew was ready as well. Gary pinpointed the course of the incoming Megalodon targeting the ship, and Martin's weapons officer met the creature with a volley of torpedoes that reduced the shark's face to pulp. Leaking blood, the shark's corpse thudded against the hull of *The 2112* carried on forward by its previous momentum. *The 2112* shuddered from the blow but held together, mostly undamaged.

"Captain!" Gary shouted at her. "All but three ships of the Fleet have been destroyed. The Megalodons are circling around for another run!"

Captain Martin heard the fear in Gary's voice. It was clear the sonar tech wanted her to give the order for them to run. She couldn't though.

"How many of the Megalodons are left?" Martin snapped.

"I can't get a good read on them. There's too much debris in the water."

"Best guess!"

"Nine," Gary answered.

The 2112's helmsman whirled around at his station to confront Martin. "Captain, we've got to make a run for it!"

Captain Martin had to respect the man for having the balls to challenge her and say what everyone else had to be thinking.

"No," Martin snarled. "There's nowhere to run to. We make our stand here."

"For the Fleet!" Gary yelled, lending her some support though his voice was strained.

"For the Fleet!" the rest of the crew on the bridge other than the helmsman echoed.

The other two remaining ships of the Fleet were between the herd of Megalodons and *The 2112*. Captain Martin watched the sharks plow through them. Two more Megalodons met their death. It was a true credit to the captains of those last two vessels. Then there was no time for anything but barking orders and silent prayers.

The 2112 opened up with everything she had. Deck mounted guns blazed at the incoming sharks. Torpedoes hit the water, streaking towards the monsters. Some members of the crew that were topside even fired their personal weapons into the waves. The sharks came straight on into the fury that met them. Another two Megalodons were sent to Hell before three of the creatures struck the ship in unison. Captain Martin remained defiant to the end. She, too, had rigged her ship for the worst. All throughout *The 2112* its crew had scrambled to place charges. Captain Martin was flung to the floor of the bridge by the sharks' impact, but her thumb shoved down the button of the detonator she clutched. *The 2112* blew apart, taking all three of the Megalodons with her in a blaze of glory.

****

The battle was over, and the war was lost. Admiral Campbell had watched *The 2112's* brave, final sacrifice from one of Dry Dock's lookout towers. The Fleet, his fleet, was gone. The only boats left to the city of Dry Dock were its lifeboats, and they were useless with the sharks out there beneath the waves, waiting. The Helo that been dispatched earlier had returned safely, and for that Admiral Campbell was thankful, though in the great scheme of things, it mattered little. The platform city's two Helos lacked the range to be of any real use to the city in terms of gathering supplies or performing the other long range functions that his fleet would have carried out for the city had they survived. Dry Dock was the most self-sustaining cluster of humanity that remained in the world, but even it couldn't last forever on its own.

Admiral Campbell wiped tears from his cheeks with the backside of his hands and turned away from the horizon. Goh was there waiting on him.

"We have the fires in the city under control. As you know, the terrorist-like attack of the two Hordesmen and Serena did very little damage to anything other than the citizens of Dry Dock and their homes. Our labs, production facilities, and farms are all intact," Goh told him.

"Good work," Campbell managed to say with a quick nod. He left Goh standing on the open lookout portion of the tower and headed down its stairs. There was no point in looking out to the waves anymore. They were cut off from mankind now. The Megalodons owned them now and had taken their rightful place as the rulers of the ocean. All that was left now was the city and its uncertain future. Campbell promised himself he would find a way to keep things going aboard it and its survivors alive.

END

Eric S Brown is the author of numerous series including the Bigfoot War series, the Kaiju Apocalypse series (Jason Cordova), the Homeworld series, the Crypto-Squad series (with Jason Brannon), the Jack Bunny Bam Bam series, and the A Pack of Wolves series. Some of his standalone books include Megalodon, Megalodons, War of the Worlds Plus Blood Guts and Zombies, Sasquatch Lake, Kaiju Armageddon, Dawn of the Kaiju, Night of the Kaiju, The Weaponer, Last Stand in a Dead Land, and World War of the Dead to name only a few. Eric's short fiction has been published hundreds of times in the small press and beyond including markets such as Baen Book's Onward Drake anthology, The Grantville Gazette, Walmart World Magazine, and the SNAFU anthology series. He also writes an ongoing comic book/pop culture news column entitled "Comics in a Flash" for The Guide. The first book of his Bigfoot War series was produced as a major motion picture in 2014 staring C. Thomas Howell and Judd Nelson. His book The Witch of Devil's Woods (co-authored by James Baack) was also made into a feature film and released in 2015. At this time, a 3rd adaptation of one of Brown's books in production and slated for a 2016 release. Eric lives in western North Carolina with his wife and two children where he continues to write tales of blazing guns, the hungry dead, and the monsters that lurk in the woods.

CHECK OUT OTHER GREAT
DEEP SEA THRILLERS

MEGA
by Jake Bible

There is something in the deep. Something large. Something hungry. Something prehistoric.
And Team Grendel must find it, fight it, and kill it.
Kinsey Thorne, the first female US Navy SEAL candidate has hit rock bottom. Having washed out of the Navy, she turned to every drink and drug she could get her hands on. Until her father and cousins, all ex-Navy SEALS themselves, offer her a way back into the life: as part of a private, elite combat Team being put together to find and hunt down an impossible monster in the Indian Ocean. Kinsey has a second chance, but can she live through it?

THE BLACK
by Paul E Cooley

Under 30,000 feet of water, the exploration rig Leaguer has discovered an oil field larger than Saudi Arabia, with oil so sweet and pure, nations would go to war for the rights to it. But as the team starts drilling exploration well after exploration well in their race to claim the sweet crude, a deep rumbling beneath the ocean floor shakes them all to their core. Something has been living in the oil and it's about to give birth to the greatest threat humanity has ever seen.

"The Black" is a techno/horror-thriller that puts the horror and action of movies such as Leviathan and The Thing right into readers' hands. Ocean exploration will never be the same."

CHECK OUT OTHER GREAT DEEP SEA THRILLERS

PREDATOR X
by C.J Waller

When deep level oil fracking uncovers a vast subterranean sea, a crack team of cavers and scientists are sent down to investigate. Upon their arrival, they disappear without a trace. A second team, including sedimentologist Dr Megan Stoker, are ordered to seek out Alpha Team and report back their findings. But Alpha team are nowhere to be found – instead, they are faced with something unexpected in the depths. Something ancient. Something huge. Something dangerous. Predator X

DEAD BAIT
by Tim Curran

A husband hell-bent on revenge hunts a Wereshark...A Russian mail order bride with a fishy secret...Crabs with a collective consciousness...A vampire who transforms into a Candiru...Zombie piranha...Bait that will have you crawling out of your skin and more. Drawing on horror, humor with a helping of dark fantasy and a touch of deviance, these 19 contemporary stories pay homage to the monsters that lurk in the murky waters of our imaginations. If you thought it was safe to go back in the water...Think Again!

LAMPREYS
by Alan Spencer

A secret government tactical team is sent to perform a clean sweep of a private research installation. Horrible atrocities lurk within the abandoned corridors. Mutated sea creatures with insane killing abilities are waiting to suck the blood and meat from their prey.
Unemployed college professor Conrad Garfield is forced to assist and is soon separated from the team. Alone and afraid, Conrad must use his wits to battle mutated lampreys, infected scientists and go head-to-head with the biggest monstrosity of all.
Can Conrad survive, or will the deadly monsters suck the very life from his body?

DEEP DEVOTION
by M.C. Norris

Rising from the depths, a mind-bending monster unleashes a wave of terror across the American heartland. Kate Browning, a Kansas City EMT confronts her paralyzing fear of water when she traces the source of a deadly parasitic affliction to the Gulf of Mexico. Cooperating with a marine biologist, she travels to Florida in an effort to save the life of one very special patient, but the source of the epidemic happens to be the nest of a terrifying monster, one that last rose from the depths to annihilate the lost continent of Atlantis.

Leviathan, destroyer, devoted lifemate and parent, the abomination is not going to take the extermination of its brood well.

www.ingramcontent.com/pod-product-compliance
Lightning Source LLC
Chambersburg PA
CBHW030513130626
46549CB00007B/2974